NBA HIGHLIGHT REEL

by John Hareas

T5-DHH-317

Scholastic Inc.

New York   Toronto   London   Auckland   Sydney
Mexico City   New Delhi   Hong Kong   Buenos Aires

To Emma, Chris, and Leah.
Thank you for making me so proud.
– Love, DAD

Photos:

Front cover (left to right): Garrett Ellwood; Issac Baldizon; Ron Turenne

Back cover (left to right): Gary Dineen; Noah Graham; Nathaniel S. Butler

Interior: (4-5) Issac Baldizon; (6-7) Jesse D. Garrabrant; (8-9, 10-11, 20-21) Andrew D. Bernstein; (12) Gary Dineen; (13) Garrett Ellwood; (14-15) Melissa Majchrzak; (16-17, 23) Noah Graham; (18-19) Nathaniel S. Butler; (22) Kent Smith; (24-25) Ron Turenne; (26-27) Fernando Medina; (28-29) Paul Chapman; (30) Sam Forencich; (31) Kent Smith; (32) Ned Dishman

ISBN-13: 978-0-545-09416-0
ISBN-10: 0-545-09416-X

12 11 10 9 8 7 6 5 4 3 2 1   9 10 11/0

Printed in the U.S.A.
First printing, January 2009

Intro

How cool would it be to sit courtside and watch Kobe Bryant hit a playoff game-winning jumper with only seconds remaining on the game clock? Or watch as LeBron James scores 25 straight points against one of the NBA's premier defensive teams, the Detroit Pistons, and single-handedly leads the Cavaliers to one of the biggest playoff wins in franchise history? Imagine sitting under the basket as Robert Horry of the San Antonio Spurs silences more than 22,000 fans in a split second as he drains a three-pointer with 5.8 seconds remaining in Game 5 of the NBA Finals. A game that featured 18 ties!

In this book you'll have a front-row seat for some of the greatest and most thrilling clutch baskets from the last few seasons. Learn how some of the NBA's premier players were able to perform, and most importantly deliver, under pressure. Great moments aren't reserved for the stars only. Role players play a big part in a team's success, too, as you'll see in the following pages. So, sit back and enjoy reading about these amazing moments and in no time, you'll be creating some Highlight Reel moves of your own!

Frantic Finish

Who do you call when you're 17 points down? Dwyane Wade. In February 2006, the All-Star guard scored 17 straight points including a 16-foot shot with 2.3 seconds remaining as the Miami Heat led the Detroit Pistons, 100–98. "Dwyane took the game over," Detroit coach Flip Saunders said. No doubt.

Agent Zero Delivers!

When Gilbert Arenas isn't blogging for NBA.com, he is hitting game-winning shots like this one over Kirk Hinrich and Tyson Chandler of the Chicago Bulls in Game 5 of the 2005 Eastern Conference Semifinals. Arenas's basket not only silenced the enthusiastic Bulls fans but gave the Wizards a 112–110 win. How big was the basket? It gave the Wizards a 3–2 series lead and ultimately the first-round victory over the Bulls.

Game Winner? Bank It!

Game 6 of the 2005 First Round match-up between the San Antonio Spurs and Seattle SuperSonics appeared headed into overtime. Apparently, Tim Duncan had other ideas. The future Hall of Famer received the ball, swiftly positioned himself near the basket, and banked a short shot with 0.5 seconds remaining to end the game — and the Sonics' season. Duncan and the Spurs were on their way to the franchise's third championship.

Big Shot Bob
Strikes Again!

I t was one of the greatest clutch shots in NBA Finals history. Robert Horry scored all 21 of his points in the second half of Game 5 of the 2005 NBA Finals. Yet the basket that loomed the largest was the game-winning three-pointer with 5.8 seconds remaining that stunned the sold-out Palace crowd. The

Spurs defeated the Pistons 96–95, and it was a dramatic ending to a very close game. How close? It was a game that saw 12 lead changes and 18 ties. For Horry, it was yet another clutch basket in a career filled with them.

t was Michael Redd's first buzzer-beater of his NBA career — and most likely it won't be his last. It was February 26, 2008. LeBron James and the Cleveland Cavaliers were visiting (playing Cleveland is always extra special for Redd, who grew up in Columbus, Ohio). After James hit the game-tying layup, Redd dribbled quickly up the court only to be stopped by Cavalier Wally Szczerbiak. Redd was forced to throw up a 27-foot shot that sailed right through the hoop. The buzzer sounded and the Bucks won 105–102. "The shot felt good all the way going up," Redd said. "And I was happy it went in." So were the Buck fans.

Carmelo Anthony is used to playing in big moments. As a freshman, Anthony led Syracuse University to the national title. Against the Phoenix Suns, Anthony proved why he is a rising NBA star. In January 2006, the Nuggets and the Suns were entangled in a close — and intense — game. How intense? Anthony got kneed in the face during one play but refused to be taken out. Good thing for the Nuggets, because Melo ended up scoring 43 points — including the game-winning jumper — to give Denver a thrilling 139–137 triple-overtime victory.

A Melo–morable Performance

Pile On!

The Nets celebrated in euphoric fashion after Vince Carter shocked the Jazz and its home crowd with a late January 2007 gem. The Nets were trailing 115–113 when Carter received the inbounds pass with only 5.9 seconds remaining. He dribbled beyond halfcourt and pulled up about seven feet behind the three point line where he launched a three-pointer that swished — with only two seconds remaining on the clock!

Kobe—rriffic!

A big-game player loves big-game moments, and no one does it better at the end of a game than Kobe Bryant. The All-Star guard drained a 17-foot jumper as the buzzer sounded to give the Lakers a thrilling 99–98 victory over the Phoenix Suns in Game 4 of the 2006 Western Conference Semifinals.

Bold Shot

Damon Jones calls himself the "best shooter in the universe," and against the Washington Wizards in Game 6 of the First Round of the 2006 NBA Playoffs, he certainly lived up to that self-proclaimed billing. On the road, Jones nailed a 17-footer with 4.8 seconds in overtime to give the Cavs a 114–113 win and its first playoff series victory in 13 years!

Derek Fisher's
0.4 Miracle Shot

For Derek Fisher, May 13, 2004 is a day he will always remember. It was Game 5 of the Western Conference Semifinals, and Tim Duncan had hit a sensational off-balance 20-foot fadeaway over the Lakers' Shaquille O'Neal with 0.4 seconds remaining. The Spurs were in good shape to win, right? After all, there was only time for one quick play, and what were the chances the Lakers would win the game with only 0.4 seconds remaining? Well, that was all the time Derek Fisher needed as he received the inbound pass and looped an 18-foot turnaround swish over Manu Ginobili to seal the Lakers' unlikely comeback victory.

Ray Allen
Game Winner

Nothing was going right for Ray Allen. *Clang . . . Clang . . . Clang*. Ray missed 11 of 14 shots against the Charlotte Bobcats in this late November 2007 game. Despite his off night, guess who wanted the ball when it was crunch time? You guessed it, Ray Allen. Once a shooter, always a shooter, and Ray didn't disappoint, hitting a nothing-but-net buzzer-beating three-pointer. Final Score: Celtics 96, Bobcats 95.

Stackhouse to the Rescue!

It was January 2008, and the Mavericks' six-game winning streak appeared to be over. Visiting the Clippers in Los Angeles, Dallas was down by two with only seconds remaining. The Mavs were on the verge of their first loss in seven games when suddenly Jerry Stackhouse rescued them from the jaws of defeat. He nailed a three-pointer as the buzzer sounded, giving the Mavs a thrilling 95–94 victory and their seventh win in a row!

Ray Rocks the Raptors

November 4, 2007: It was only game two of Ray Allen's Boston Celtic career, and what a memorable game it was! With the Celtics and Raptors locked in a 95–95 tie, Allen broke free from his defender as teammate Paul Pierce passed him the ball. As the clock wound down to zero, Allen nailed a three-pointer from the corner with less than three seconds remaining. The Celtics ended up winning, 98–95. Welcome to the Celtics, Ray!

Hedo! Hedo!

I n 2007–08 Hedo Turkoglu was enjoying the best season of his NBA career, so it wasn't any surprise that he would create one of his most memorable moments during that time. With the Boston Celtics visiting and boasting the league's best record, the game was tied 93–93. Turkoglu needed to produce a little Magic of his own to deliver an Orlando victory. As the clock was set to expire, Turkoglu heaved an off-balance 25-foot three-pointer at the buzzer and *POOF!* — the Celtics lost to the Magic, 96-93.

Touching the Clouds

February 9, 2007: How impressive was Dwight Howard's first ever game-winning dunk over Tim Duncan and the San Antonio Spurs with 0.2 seconds remaining? Just ask Spur Brent Barry: "Dwight had to go up and touch the clouds over Timmy, and get it one-handed and put it in. It was a remarkable play." And a remarkable victory for the Orlando Magic, 106–104.

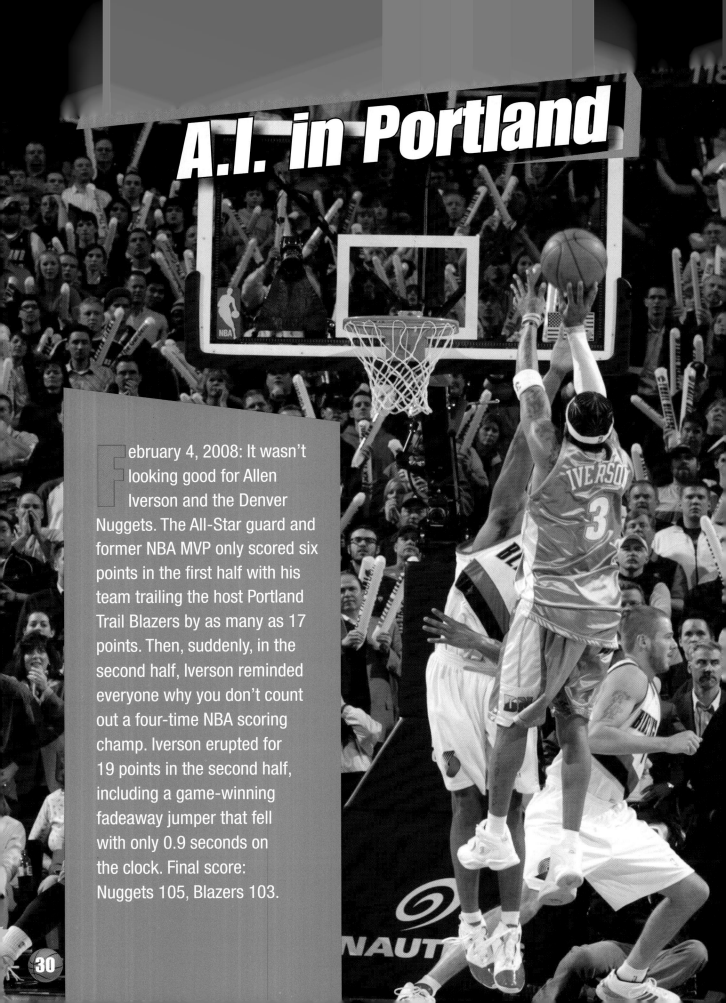

A.I. in Portland

February 4, 2008: It wasn't looking good for Allen Iverson and the Denver Nuggets. The All-Star guard and former NBA MVP only scored six points in the first half with his team trailing the host Portland Trail Blazers by as many as 17 points. Then, suddenly, in the second half, Iverson reminded everyone why you don't count out a four-time NBA scoring champ. Iverson erupted for 19 points in the second half, including a game-winning fadeaway jumper that fell with only 0.9 seconds on the clock. Final score: Nuggets 105, Blazers 103.

Rookie Delivers a Veteran Performance

On November 16, 2007 his NBA career was only 10 games old, but that didn't stop rookie Kevin Durant from making an impression. With the Hawks and Sonics tied at 123, Durant had the ball — and the Sonics' chance at victory. So what did Durant do? He faked out his defender, rookie Al Horford, with a pump fake and then faded for a three-pointer from the top of the key. He swished it for a 126–123 double-overtime Sonics victory. "This is what I live for," Durant said after the game. "I wouldn't have it any other way."

LeBron's
Instant Playoff Classic

May 31, 2007: Mark it down as the official date LeBron James became a great NBA player. The scene: Game 5 of the 2007 Eastern Conference Finals. With the Cavaliers trailing 87–81 and a little over three minutes to play, LeBron went on a tear, scoring 25 consecutive points as the game went into double overtime. LeBron (who else?) eventually scored the game-winning layup as the Cavaliers downed the Pistons in one of the greatest playoff performances of all time!